Never Enough Hockey!

by
Gilles Tibo

illustrations by
Bruno St-Aubin

Scholastic Canada Ltd.
Toronto New York London Auckland Sydney
Mexico City New Delhi Hong Kong Buenos Aires

Scholastic Canada Ltd.
604 King Street West, Toronto, Ontario M5V 1E1, Canada

Scholastic Inc.
557 Broadway, New York, NY 10012, USA

Scholastic Australia Pty Limited
PO Box 579, Gosford, NSW 2250, Australia

Scholastic New Zealand Limited
Private Bag 94407, Botany, Manukau 2163, New Zealand

Scholastic Children's Books
Euston House, 24 Eversholt Street, London NW1 1DB, UK

www.scholastic.ca

Library and Archives Canada Cataloguing in Publication

Tibo, Gilles, 1951-
[À l'entraînement, Nicolas! English]
Never enough hockey! / Gilles Tibo ; illustrations by Bruno St-Aubin ;
translated by Petra Johannson.

Translation of: À l'entraînement, Nicolas!
ISBN 978-1-4431-5566-3 (softcover)

I. St-Aubin, Bruno, illustrator II. Johannson, Petra, translator
III. Title. IV. Title: À l'entraînement, Nicolas! English.

PS8589.I26A62813 2017   jC843'.54   C2017-901460-9

6 5 4 3 2 1   Printed in Malaysia 108   17 18 19 20 21

At the crack of dawn, Nicholas's dad
came running into his bedroom.

"Quick, Nicholas! Get dressed! Hockey
camp starts today!"

But Nicholas couldn't even lift his head. His dad felt his forehead, then ran out and got a thermometer. Nicholas's teeth chattered as he held it under his tongue.

"Nicholas, you have a very high fever! You need to stay in bed."

"Oh no!" Nicholas groaned. "What about training camp?"

Nicholas knew he was really sick because his dad, his mom and even his sister were not joking about it at all. One, two, three, four, five, six long days passed with his family pampering him.

He rested, took his medicine, drank lots
of water. While all his friends were at
hockey camp, Nicholas watched movies
with his cat. He wondered if he would
ever feel better.

Finally, on the seventh day, Nicholas woke up feeling great.

His dad was just hanging up the phone in the kitchen.

"Nicholas, I have bad news and good news," he said.

"Start with the bad news," Nicholas said.

"Unfortunately, it's too late to join the training camp."

"WHAT?" said Nicholas. "What's the good news?"

"Coach said you can try out with everyone else in a week. If you qualify, you can be part of the team."

"But I'll have missed all the training! How will I keep up with everyone?" Nicholas was completely discouraged.

He sat down to eat his cereal and announced: "I've had enough of hockey. I think I'd like to try another sport!"

His parents just stared in stunned silence.

"Other sport?" asked his sister. "What other sport?"

Nicholas grabbed the phone. Since all
his hockey friends were at training camp,
he called on other friends.

An hour later, Nicholas headed out with his dad's old tennis racquet. He met up with Maddy, the tennis champion. Maddy gave Nicholas tips. She encouraged him. Nicholas improved. He played and played and played.

But at the end of the day, his arms felt like spaghetti. Tennis was not for him.

The next day at the park, Nicholas tried gymnastics with Dominick. Dom gave Nicholas tips. He encouraged him. Nicholas improved. He somersaulted, spun and even did a backflip.

But at the end of the day, he was so
dizzy he didn't even know where he lived.
Gymnastics was not for him.

The next day, Nicholas went running
with Julie. Julie gave Nicholas tips.
She encouraged him. Nicholas improved.
He was sprinting like a leopard.
He was running like a gazelle.

But at the end of the day, he had
cramps in his thighs, calves and toes.
Running was not for him.

The next day, Nicholas played table tennis with Kim. Kim gave Nicholas tips. She encouraged him. Nicholas improved. His reflexes were as fast as lightning. He returned every shot.

PONG!

But at the end of the day, Nicholas was so tired he collapsed on the floor. Table tennis was not for him.

The next day, Nicholas tried lifting weights with William. William gave Nicholas tips. He encouraged him. Nicholas improved. He was lifting weights as heavy as elephants.

But at the end of the day, Nicholas's muscles were sore and blown up like balloons. Weightlifting was not for him.

The next day, Nicholas tried yoga with Agnes to improve his concentration. But he would never be as flexible as her.

That afternoon, Nicholas tried diving with Diego, and found out he was afraid of heights.

That evening, he went swimming with Max and learned that he liked water, but he loved ice. Especially ice rinks. He really missed playing hockey. And the tryouts were the next day!

Nicholas was so nervous he didn't sleep at all. Early the next morning he put on his goalie equipment. On the way to the arena, his dad gave Nicholas tips. He encouraged him. He told Nicholas he was the best goalie in the world. But Nicholas had zero confidence.

Soon, with his heart racing, Nicholas was out on the ice with the rest of the players. There were three other goalies! They were big. And tall. They looked mean.

The three other goalies took their turns in net. They had all the moves. They stopped almost every shot on goal. Nicholas's confidence sank even lower.

The coach blew the whistle. It was Nicholas's turn to take shots on goal. He was shaking all over. The players came forward, ready to attack.

Nicholas trembled with fear.

And then, it clicked. Using a yogi's concentration and the strength of a weightlifter, Nicholas somersaulted, spun and did backflips. With the flexibility of a gymnast, the precision of a tennis player and the speed of a runner, he stopped every single puck!

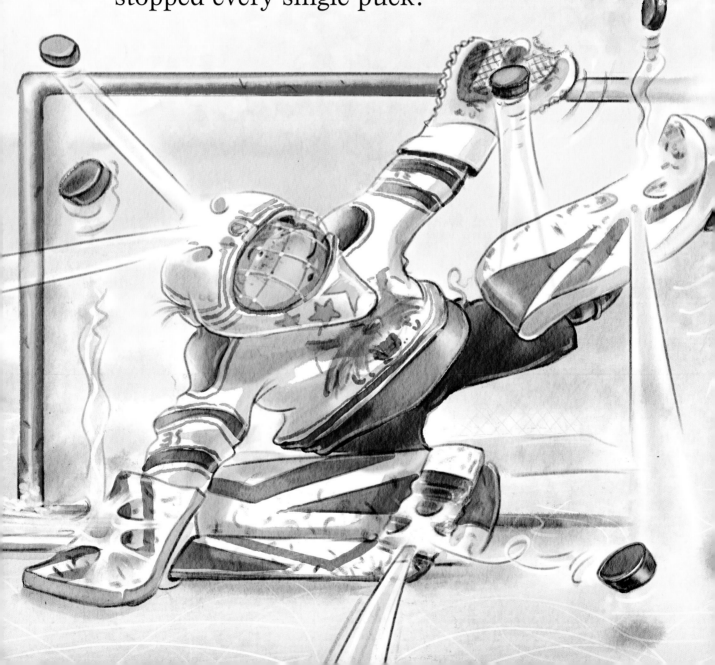

Nicholas would be the starting
goalie! He got a standing ovation.
    "What's your secret?" everyone asked.
    Nicholas answered honestly.
"My secret is . . ."

". . . my friends: Maddy, Dominick, Julie,
Kim, William, Agnes, Diego and Max!"